D0513339

Postman Pat® and the ice-Cream Machine

SIMON AND SCHUSTER

It was a hot sunny day in Greendale.

Sara and Nisha were busy in the station café when Pat and Jess arrived with the post.

"We're making sandwiches for the children's picnic at Ted's this afternoon," said Sara.

"Are you coming, Pat?" asked Nisha.

"I hope so! Come on, Jess, we'd better hurry up and get these letters delivered."

"Oh Pat, could you take this sugar over to Ted's?" asked Ajay.
"He's built an ice-cream machine. He's making ice-cream for the picnic."

"Mmm! That sounds good! No problem, Ajay."

Ted was testing his ice-cream machine.

"In with the strawberries. There we go!"

Meera and Julian were watching through the window.

"Strawberry ice-cream. Yum!"

"Let's see now, just need to plug it in. . . and switch it on. . . ."

There was a flash and a fizz and a loud bang – and Ted flew backwards through the doorway!

"Are you all right, Ted?" asked Julian and Meera.

Ted's hair was standing up on end.

"Oh aye, nowt to worry about. But the electric's gone."

"Looks like we're going to have to wait for the ice-cream," said Julian.

"Let's go and see what else we can find to make different flavours," suggested Meera.

Pat arrived at Ted's workshop with the sugar.

"Hello, Ted. How's the ice-cream going?"

"I've got a spot of bother, Pat. My power supply's broken, but I reckon you can help."

Mrs Thompson gave Julian and Meera a basket of blackcurrants.

"Thanks! These will make great ice-cream!"

"Cherries are good in ice-cream, too," said Bill.

"Good idea!" said Meera. "Reverend Timms has a cherry tree in his garden. Let's go and ask him."

Pat and Ted connected up the wires from Pat's van to the ice-cream machine.

"Ready, Ted?" Pat revved up the engine.

The ice-cream maker started to shake and judder.

There was too much power coming from Pat's van.

A big dollop of strawberry ice-cream flew out of the machine. . .

. . . just as PC Selby was riding past on his bicycle.

SPLAT! The ice-cream landed on PC Selby's helmet.

"Oi! Where did that come from?"

"What's going on here?" asked PC Selby, as the strawberry ice-cream ran down his face.

"It's a VERY serious, mmm, strawberry, a very serious mmmmm, won't do at all, mmmm tasty."

"Sorry, PC Selby, Pat was helping me get my ice-cream maker working. But his van is a bit too powerful for the job. We'll have to try something else."

"I have an idea!" said Pat. "PC Selby's bike!"

Meanwhile, Reverend Timms picked a whole basket of delicious cherries for Meera and, by early afternoon, the children had also collected some bananas, a bag of toffees, some walnuts. . .

and something very special from Mrs Goggins!

PC Selby pedalled until he was red in the face.
The ice-cream machine was turning slowly,
but the mixture wasn't getting cold enough.

"We need more power," said Pat. "I know! Solar power!"

Ted and Pat nailed Ted's solar panels to the roof.
The panels made electricity from the sun, and the
ice-cream machine sprang into life!

"We did it, Ted!" beamed Pat. "And now I'd better get on with my
deliveries!"

"Tell you what, Pat, I'll give you a hand. One good turn deserves
another!"

So Pat and Ted set off to finish Pat's round, leaving PC Selby in charge.

PC Selby was tired out from all his pedalling.
He fell fast asleep, while the machine whirred and hummed . . .
and strawberry ice-cream oozed out onto the floor . . . .

Julian, Meera and Bill headed for Ted's with their bags,
baskets and the big blue pot.

Jess was very interested in the blue pot!

When Pat and Ted got back, there was ice-cream everywhere! But they soon had everything cleaned up and Ted made some final adjustments to the machine. Then he put in the cream and sugar, but he had completely run out of strawberries.

"Oh no! What are we going to do?"

The children arrived just in time!

"Don't worry, Mr Glen," said Julian. "We've got loads of other ingredients."

"By gum. I reckon you kids have just about saved the day!" smiled Ted.

"Right now, let's get on with it!" chuckled Ted. "Which flavour first?"
"Banana and toffee please," the children agreed.

"What's in the blue pot, Julian?" Pat asked.

"It's a surprise, Dad," replied Julian, "for someone very special."

Everybody tucked into the ice-cream.

"Mmmm, delicious!"

"I'll have some of the special surprise one, please!" Pat said, taking a big mouthful from the blue pot before Julian could stop him.

"Dad!" Julian laughed, as Pat spluttered. "It's not meant for people. It's a special SARDINE ice-cream for Jess!"

Everyone laughed, as Jess licked happily. "Miaow!"

SIMON AND SCHUSTER
First published in 2004 in Great Britain by Simon & Schuster UK Ltd
Africa House, 64-78 Kingsway
London WC2B 6AH
A CBS COMPANY

This hardback edition published in 2007

Postman Pat® © 2004 Woodland Animations, a division of Entertainment Rights PLC
Licensed by Entertainment Rights PLC
Original writer John Cunliffe
From the original television design by Ivor Wood
Royal Mail and Post Office imagery is used by kind permission of Royal Mail Group plc
All rights reserved

Text by Alison Ritchie © 2004 Simon & Schuster UK Ltd

All rights reserved including the right of reproduction in whole or in part in any form

A CIP catalogue record for this book is available from the British Library upon request

ISBN-10: 1-84738-080-8
ISBN-13: 978-1-84738-080-7

Printed in China
1 3 5 7 9 10 8 6 4 2